CLASS PETS

Battle in a Bottle

FRANK ASCH

Illustrated by John Kanzler

SIMON & SCHUSTER BOOKS FOR YOUNG READERS

NEW YORK   LONDON   TORONTO   SYDNEY   SINGAPORE

SIMON & SCHUSTER BOOKS FOR YOUNG READERS
An imprint of Simon & Schuster Children's Publishing Division
1230 Avenue of the Americas, New York, New York 10020
Text copyright © 2003 by Frank Asch
Illustrations copyright © 2003 by John Kanzler
All rights reserved, including the right of reproduction in whole or in
part in any form.
SIMON & SCHUSTER BOOKS FOR YOUNG READERS is a trademark of
Simon & Schuster.
Book design by O'Lanso Gabbidon
The text for this book is set in Trump Mediaeval.
The illustrations for this book are rendered in pencil.
Manufactured in the United States of America
2 4 6 8 10 9 7 5 3 1
Library of Congress Cataloging-in-Publication Data
Asch, Frank.
Battle in a bottle / Frank Asch ; illustrated by John Kanzler.
p. cm. — (Class pets)
Summary: Molly and Jake begin to settle into their new home in
Public School Forty-two, behind the nail hole in Miss Clark's room.
ISBN 0-689-84655-X
[1. Mice—Fiction. 2. Schools—Fiction.] I. Kanzler, John, ill. II.
Title.
PZ7.A778 Bcm 2003
[Fic]—dc21
2002006113

To my cousin Rose, who once had a pet squirrel—F. A.

For Diane—J. K.

Chapter 1

Molly and Peaches had just met the night before, but already they greeted each other like old friends, with a nose touch.

"How was your first day at P.S. Forty-two?" asked Peaches.

"Terrific!" exclaimed Molly. "I really love it here. But sleeping was a bit drafty inside the wall. When I woke up, my nose was cold."

"Well, that's just—"

Suddenly Peaches turned the pink of her long ears toward the classroom windows. "Hear that?"

Molly quieted her mind and listened.

"All I hear is a paper bag blowing across the playground," said Molly. "And . . ." Molly's eyes grew wide and alert. ". . . *cat's paws on pavement!* Could that be? . . ."

"You got it!' said Peaches. "Big Gray is on the prowl tonight!"

The mere mention of Big Gray's name set Molly's heart thumping like a tiny jackhammer.

"Are you sure it's him?"

Peaches nodded gravely. "I'm afraid so, dear. But don't worry. You'll be safe as long as you stay inside."

"Hey, Jake!" Molly called to her brother.

At that moment Jake was on the other side of the class-pet table watching guppies swim round and round in lazy circles. The back and forth swish of their tails and fins, and the green glow of the aquarium light had put him into a kind of trance.

"Huh?" he said without looking up.

"Over here!" called Molly. "It's important!"

Jake tore himself away from the guppies and sauntered over to Peaches' cage.

"Good to see you again," said Peaches with a courteous nod.

"Yeah," mumbled Jake.

Though brother and sister, Jake and Molly looked very different. Molly's fur was a slightly grayish color. Jake's was almost chocolate brown. Molly was small and thin with tiny ears, delicate features, and long, even whiskers. Jake was big and chubby with large leafy ears and short, crooked whiskers.

They were different in other ways too.

When Jake heard the news about Big Gray, he just shrugged. "That old mop doesn't scare me!" he boasted. "I outsmarted him last night, and if I have to, I'll outsmart him again tonight!"

"Oh, Jake," exclaimed Molly. "It worries me to hear you talk like that. Promise me you won't go outside tonight."

"Don't worry, Sis. We're making our nests tonight, remember?"

"Making nests?" asked Peaches. "Does that mean you're moving into P.S. Forty-two for good?"

"Oh, yes!" piped Molly. "Isn't it wonderful?"

"Hold on a mousy minute!" Jake brought a rear leg up to scratch behind an ear. "I never agreed to stay for good. Only to try it out."

"Yes! Yes! I know," declared Molly. "But you're going to *love* it here. I just know you are!"

"Maybe, maybe not," Jake slowly shook his head from side to side. "I'll tell you one thing. The old plaster walls in this place are, as Poppa would say, 'drafty as a slice of Swiss cheese.'"

"A nice cozy nest will fix that problem," said Peaches as she hopped over to her water bowl and took a drink.

"That's right," agreed Molly. "Like Momma always said, 'a house without a nest is not a home.'"

"Perhaps you two would like some of my cedar shavings for your nests?" offered the plump white rabbit. "My cage was cleaned this afternoon, so I've got a *fresh* supply."

Molly was just about to accept Peaches' offer when Jake spoke up.

"Thanks, but no thanks!" he said, sounding almost snippy.

Molly was stunned. "What are you talking about? Of course, we'd *love* some cedar shavings!" she exclaimed. "They smell so sweet!"

"Yeah, but we don't need them," said Jake. "Just look around. There's enough paper in this classroom to make a hundred nests."

"But paper is *so* ordinary!" declared Molly. "I want my first nest in my first real home to be *special.* Besides, we're not living in a deli anymore, Jake. This is a *school!* Paper is important here."

"Molly's right," said Peaches with a wink. "You wouldn't want to chew up someone's homework to make your nest. Would you?"

3

"Sure, why not?" answered Jake. "We're mice. Chewing things up is what we do best!"

"Speak for yourself!" gasped Molly. "Personally, I wouldn't dream of gnawing on anything that belonged to Miss Clark or one of her kids. Not to mention the fact that it would be like leaving a note that said, 'Yoo-hoo! It's us, the mice. We're moving in!'"

"So we take the paper from the wastepaper basket," said Jake. "That way nobody's feelings get hurt."

Molly squeaked a high-pitched yip. "Jake, I'm surprised at you! How many times did Momma and Poppa tell us never to go near wastepaper baskets?"

"Yeah, I know." Jake recited the rhyme his parents made all their offspring memorize:

> "The wastepaper basket
> Is a mouse's casket.
> Jump and shout and thrash about.
> Once you fall in, you never get out!"

"And what about Uncle Benny?" Molly reminded Jake of the horror story Poppa often told about his kid brother who starved to death at the bottom of a wastepaper basket.

"Yeah, yeah, but—"

Suddenly a rumbling could be heard from Jake's belly. It got louder and louder until . . .

"B-U-U-U-R-R-R-P! Wow! That's got to be the loudest burp I ever made!" Jake grinned proudly. "Too bad I wasn't in a burp contest right now. I'd win *first* prize!"

"Too bad you never paid attention when Momma tried to teach you some manners," quipped Molly.

"So, are either of you interested in any of my cedar shavings?" asked Peaches.

"I am!" said Molly.

"How about you, Jake?" asked Peaches.

Jake heaved a huge sigh. He wanted to build his own nest in his *own* way. But he did like the smell of cedar shavings. As a matter of fact, he loved it.

"Sure, why not?" He shrugged.

"Then it's settled," said Peaches. "Just open my cage door and I'll kick some out for both of you."

A single block of pine kept Peaches' door shut. But neither Jake nor Molly, nor the both of them working together, could budge it.

"Don't worry," said Peaches. "We'll just call Gino. He opens my cage all the time."

"That old spook?" asked Jake with a grimace. "Do we have to?"

"Why not?" answered Peaches. "He'll probably drop by soon anyway."

"Where is that scruffy old ghost?" wondered Molly out loud. "I haven't seen him since lunchtime."

"Why, I'm right here," announced a voice from above.

Molly and Jake looked up and saw a mist hovering over their heads. While they watched, the mist condensed into a brownish lump. Then the lump morphed into a shaggy hamster with a big grin on his face.

"Hi Gino!" cried Molly. "How are things in Hamster Heaven?"

"Couldn't be better," answered Gino as he slowly descended to the class-pet table.

Chapter 2

Gino had no trouble opening Peaches' cage. He just drifted over to the block of pine and touched it with his paw. Then he sat back and watched while it turned all by itself.

Sometimes Gino seemed so ordinary. No different, in fact, from any of Molly's uncles that lived at Deli Dan's. At other times his strange ways were absolutely astonishing.

"Gino, how do you do that?" asked Molly even before the pine block stopped turning.

"Darned if I know," Gino answered with a sly smile. "I'm still kind of new at this, you know."

Gino had lived on Miss Clark's class-pet table for many years. When he died last spring of old age, he missed being a class pet so much he decided to come back as a ghost. Now he divided his time between his lovely villa in Hamster Heaven and P.S. 42.

As soon as the door was open, Jake rushed in, took a drink from Peaches' water bowl, and started shoving cedar shavings in his mouth.

Molly was much more respectful of Peaches' home.

"May I come in?" she asked.

"But of course!" replied Peaches. *"Mi casa es su casa."*

"What does that mean?" mumbled Jake through a

mouthful of shavings that made him look like a squirrel with puffed-out cheeks.

"It means 'my cage is your cage,'" replied Peaches. "Would either of you two like a little something to eat? I've got some terrific-tasting beet greens in my food dish tonight."

"That's okay," said Molly. "We had a feast of beans and macaroni before we came to visit you. You know—the ones the kids used today to make necklaces in art class? Miss Clark made them clean up, but lots fell under the art cabinet."

"How about you, Jake? Are you hungry?" asked Peaches.

"Actually I'm stuffed." Jake spit out a wad of cedar shavings and patted his belly. "But I always save room for a good snack!"

"Then help yourself," offered Peaches.

While Jake snacked and Molly gathered cedar shavings, Gino made his usual rounds, checking to make sure everything was okay with all the class pets.

The guppies were fine, though a bit sluggish from over feeding. Gerald, the hermit crab, hardly said hello before complaining that his shell was too small and could Gino please help him find another one real soon. The crickets in the grass-filled mason jar were busy planning tomorrow's concert, and Emily, the turtle, was inside her shell fast asleep.

All that remained for Gino to visit was the lovebirds.

"Prince, Princess?" he called. "Are you up?"

"No, we're down," came Prince's mournful chirp

through the thin blue cloth that covered their cage.

"What?" asked Gino.

"Down. You know. *Depressed!*" squawked Princess. "So please go away and leave us alone in our *misery*. We'd rather not talk to anyone tonight."

Misery! Gino chuckled to himself, knowing how the lovebirds loved to exaggerate.

"Why so gloomy?" he asked as he slid a section of the blue cloth away from their door.

Prince and Princess sat at opposite sides of their perch. All their light green-and-melon-colored feathers drooped, making them look like two old socks with blue eyes and yellow beaks.

Princess heaved a huge sigh. "Something Miss Clark said in class today cut us to the quick."

"That doesn't sound like the Miss Clark I know," said Gino as he floated through the bars of the lovebirds' fancy bamboo cage. "What *exactly* did she say?"

"We'd rather not talk about it—" began Princess.

"—but since you asked we will," said Prince. The lovebirds often completed each other's sentences. "Today in science class Miss Clark talked about parrots. Did you know that lovebirds are parrots? And there are 353 species of parrots, which range in size from the four-inch long Pygmy Parrot to the forty-inch Macaw of Brazil?"

"No, I didn't," said Gino. "What's so horrible about that?"

"Nothing," said Prince. "I just thought it was interesting. That's all."

"Get to the point, dear," chided Princess. "Tell him the *horrible* part."

"I'm trying." Prince heaved and shuddered. "Miss Clark said that when two birds enter a breeding season as a couple, they don't have to waste time finding, courting, and fighting over mates."

"That's what we are," added Princess. "A couple."

"I know," said Gino.

Prince continued, "Couples can get right to work and build a nest. The sooner they build a nest, the sooner the mother bird can lay her eggs. The sooner the eggs hatch, the sooner the baby birds can fly and fend for themselves. That way when the rainy season comes more baby birds raised by couples survive. Then those birds tend to become couples because they have 'couple' genes from their parents. So after a time all parrots end up wanting to be part of a couple."

Gino waited, but Prince just sighed and slumped more deeply into himself.

"That's it? That's what bothered you so much?"

"Don't you get it?" said Princess. "We thought we were a couple all these years because we love one another so much. But now it turns out our love was really all about survival. If that's not a cruel joke then I don't know what is!"

"But I know you two," said Gino. "You *are* in love!"

"Apparently it only *looks* that way," said Prince. "Underneath it all we're just obeying our genes. Slaves to a vast breeding machine called 'natural selection'!"

"Oh, come on," said Gino. "It's not like that!"

"Isn't it?" said Prince, lowering his head to his breast.

"No, it's not!" insisted Gino.

"Are you saying Miss Clark was lying?" asked Princess.

"No, but take my word for it, there's more to love than genes and natural selection," declared Gino. "Don't forget. I've been to the *other side.* So I've seen firsthand how things *really* work!"

"We appreciate your trying to cheer us up," said Prince.

"We really do," agreed Princess. "But we'd like to be alone right now."

The tropical pair sighed together, raising and lowering their feathers in perfect unison.

Even in misery they stay bonded, thought Gino. *But I guess there's no way I can argue them out of their foul mood. I'll have to try a different approach.*

"Guess who's building nests tonight?" asked the resourceful ghost.

"We don't care," said Prince.

"Yes, you do," said Gino. "It's the two mice that moved in last night."

"The brother and sister who used to live in a deli?" Prince lifted his head from his breast. His eyes had become dull, but now a tiny light, like the light of a distant candle, flickered in them.

"That's right," said Gino. "Jake and Molly. And I bet they could use some help with their nests."

"We like Jake and Molly," said Princess, also perking up.

"So why don't you come out and stretch your wings tonight." Gino swung open the lovebird's door.

"I predict—no, *I promise*—you'll both feel a lot better if you do."

"You promise?" exclaimed Princess.

"Cross my heart and hope to die," swore Gino.

"But you're dead already!" twittered Prince, and Princess made a chirpy sound that was her way of laughing.

"See!" said Gino with a smile. "You're both feeling better already!"

Chapter 3

Molly was thrilled to accept the lovebirds' offer of help.

But Jake had his doubts. "How can anyone who spends all day cooing in a cage know much about nests?"

"As a matter of fact we know a great deal about nests," said Prince proudly, puffing up his feathers. "We are *birds* after all."

"That's right," chirped Princess. "And Miss Clark talks about nests every spring. Last spring she showed the class pictures of a bird that keeps its eggs warm by building its nest in a volcano! Imagine that! And did you know that eagles build nests that can weigh over two tons?"

"That's not the kind of knowledge I was thinking of," said Jake. "What I mean is, have you ever actually built a nest of your own?"

"What would be the point?" asked Prince. "We already live in a palace. A bamboo palace. Don't we dear?"

"Oh, yes! We dearly love our cage! It's every thing a bird could dream of."

"That's right," said Prince, preening a bit. "It's our dream cage."

"Well, if I ever build a cage, I'll ask for your help,"

said Jake, and he mumbled under his breath, "bird-brains!"

"Jake!" squeaked Molly. "That was rude! You should apologize at once!"

"*Sorry*," said Jake. "I take it back."

Molly could tell Jake's apology wasn't very sincere. But at least he was "trying" to be polite.

"You should be sorry!" said Prince. "We're really parrots, you know. Miss Clark said so. And parrots aren't like other birds. We have opposable toes, two each in front and back, which gives us greater dexterity." Prince lifted a pencil from the table and used it to scratch behind Princess's neck.

"Oh, dear, how delightful!" she cooed. "A little to the left, if you don't mind."

"And with greater dexterity comes greater intelligence," said Prince as he continued to scratch Princess's neck. "The fact that our brains are bigger than most birds' proves it! Miss Clark says so!"

"Some scientists believe our intelligence is on a par with dolphins and chimpanzees," added Princess. "Miss Clark said that's why we can talk like people."

"Miss Clark! Miss Clark!" grumbled Jake. "Doesn't anyone talk about anything else around here?"

"Come on, Princess. Let's go back to our cage," said Prince. "It's obvious our help isn't wanted here."

"Yes, it is!" Molly piped up. "There's plenty you can do."

"Like what?" said Jake. "We're going to build our nests inside a wall. Not much room to fly around in there. And we can find plenty of nest-building materials right here in this classroom."

"Maybe so," said Gino. "But wouldn't you like some soft grass or milkweed fluff in your nests? Prince and Princess could easily fly out an open window and . . ."

"Hold on," Peaches chimed in. "Big Gray is on the prowl tonight. I wouldn't advise anyone going outside, not even the lovebirds."

"Big Gray!" Prince ruffled his feathers so much that for a moment he looked like someone shaking a green feather duster. "I'd rather not tangle with *that* cat again!"

"I'm with you, dear," chirped Princess. "When I close my eyes I can still see that monster's long claws and gigantic teeth!"

"Sorry, Gino, but there's no way we're flying outdoors tonight!" said Prince.

"I rest my case," said Jake. "The dolphins and chimps have spoken."

"Not so fast, smarty!" Molly shot Jake a dirty rat look. "We could still use some help carting all these cedar shavings to the wall. Couldn't we?"

"Yeah, I guess so. . . ." Jake reluctantly agreed.

"Then it's settled," said the old ghost. "Here's how you can do it. . . ."

Gino's plan worked like a charm. Soon Prince and Princess, clutching tiny stacks of cedar shavings with their feet, were making trips back and forth between the class-pet table and Miss Clark's bookcase. When the moment was right, they released the cedar shavings. Down they fluttered behind the bookcase, to the gap in the molding that was the entrance to Jake and Molly's home in the wall.

As the lovebirds worked together their mood sky-rocketed. Pretty soon they were their good old, cheerful selves again, cooing and winking at each other as they flew.

"I don't care what Miss Clark says!" chirped Princess as she lifted yet another clawful of cedar shavings into the air. "You are my prince of parrots! My king of kindness! My four-toed fountain of forever friendship!"

"And you are my dewy diamond of delicious love! My perfect preening partner! My gene queen!" chimed Prince.

The happier the lovebirds felt, the more quickly their work progressed. In the time it took Jake and Molly to make just one trip from the class-pet table to the bookcase the job was done.

"That's it! We've got enough now," declared Jake.

"But we were just getting going," chirped Prince.

"Sorry, but there's just so many cedar shavings we can use," insisted Jake. "They're only for the foundation, you know."

"Jake's right," said Molly. "Cedar shavings smell great. But they're kind of scratchy to sleep on. We need some softer things now, like yarn."

"We'll find some yarn for you!" chirped Princess.

"Lots of yarn!" declared Prince.

"That's okay," said Jake. "We can manage now on our own."

But Prince and Princess were already soaring toward the classroom door.

"Back in a jiffy," chirped Princess.

"Or maybe sooner!" called Prince.

Chapter 4

Mouths stuffed with cedar shavings, P.S. 42's newest full-time residents pushed past the loose piece of molding behind Miss Clark's bookcase and bumped along in the darkness. Their nest site was high up in the wall opposite the classroom clock, so it took several minutes for them to get there. Jake, arriving first, spat out his mouthful of cedar shavings and sat down to rest.

"Dear, sweet Lumpkins," he said, mocking the way the lovebirds talked. "I adore each and every hair on your perfect, cutzie, wootzie, pootzie head, but wouldn't it be a lot smarter to build our nests *closer* to our doorway?"

"Mrm M wmmt tm me merr tmm pemm hmmm!" said Molly, forgetting her mouth was still stuffed with cedar shavings.

"*What?*" asked Jake.

"I said . . ." Molly cleared her mouth. "But I want to be near the peephole!"

The peephole was the rather large nail hole in the wall that looked out onto Miss Clark's classroom. "And please don't make fun of the lovebirds. Even if you don't like them, they *are* our new neighbors and deserve to be treated with respect!"

"I never said I didn't like them!" grumbled Jake. "I swear! Sometimes you sound just like Momma!"

"So what if I do?" snapped Molly. "If Momma were here now she'd remind you how helpful the lovebirds have been!"

"I never asked for their help!" grumbled Jake. "And I never asked for these cedar shavings either!"

"And nobody twisted your tail to take them!" Molly reminded Jake. "Peaches asked, and you said yes. Remember?"

"Yeah . . . I remember. . . ."

Removing a tiny curl of cedar from the back of his mouth, Jake stretched up and looked out the peep-hole.

"I don't see what's so special about this peephole," he complained. "All I see are lots of empty desks and chairs."

"It's not the chairs I look at," replied Molly. "It's the kids that sit in them I like to watch." Molly sat back, wet her paws with her tongue and wiped them like a washcloth over her smallish, well-rounded ears. Then she sighed. "Really, Jake, Miss Clark's kids are so *special*. The quiet ones, the sad ones, the funny ones, the clever ones, the noisy ones. Already, after just one day, I *love* them all!"

Jake didn't just roll his eyeballs, he shook them like a gambler rolling dice.

"You *love* them?"

"Uh-huh." Molly nodded up and down.

"The only kid *I* ever met, was so darn *special* he threw a stone at me," said Jake, referring to a time when he accidentally walked over the shoe of a young boy in the alley behind Deli Dan's.

"You scared that little boy!" squeaked Molly. "That's why he threw a stone at you. Besides, it's not just the kids I like to watch. It's Miss Clark. She has so many interesting things to say."

"Yeah, like what?" asked Jake.

"Well . . ." Molly thought for a moment. "Today she talked about why it gets cold in winter."

Jake grinned a superior grin.

"Heck, I already know about that! Poppa told me. He said there's a really big refrigerator downtown somewhere. Winter happens when someone leaves the door open for too long."

"That's not what Miss Clark said." Molly tisked loudly and repeated almost word for word Miss Clark's scientific explanation for the change of seasons.

"What a wacky idea!" said Jake when she finished. "If the earth spins round and round like a meat slicer, how come we don't fall off? Or even get dizzy? It doesn't make sense!"

"And a ten-story refrigerator sounds *right* to you?" squeaked Molly.

"All I know is that refrigerators are really cold," said Jake. "Remember the time Poppa got trapped in Deli Dan's cooler all night?"

"Do I?" chuckled Molly. "His lips turned blue and his teeth chattered for days. Momma said he looked like a *mice* cube."

Suddenly the mood changed as Molly and Jake quietly remembered family and friends left behind. They missed their Momma and Poppa and their brothers and sisters, and all their aunts and uncles. They even missed Deli Dan!

"Come on," said Jake. "We'd better get back to work."

Slowly, after many mouth-filled trips, the pile of shavings behind Miss Clark's bookcase grew smaller and smaller, and the pile inside the wall grew larger and larger. By 2:00 A.M. they were done.

"Now we divide them up," said Jake. "Half for me and half for you. How shall we do it?"

"Same way Momma always made us share treats," said Molly. "One of us divides. The other one picks."

"Sounds fair to me," said Jake. "You divide. I'll pick."

Molly looked at the mound of shavings and plowed right through it, creating two piles where before there was only one. Knowing Jake would want the larger pile, she made the one nearest the peephole a little smaller.

"Easy choice for me," announced Jake. "I'll take this pile. It's obviously bigger!"

"That's okay," said Molly with a smile.

"Achoo!" Jake sneezed out a cedar sliver from his nose and fell backward into a wooden beam. As his head struck the beam a round chunk of wood popped out, creating a knothole.

"Hey, Mol. Take a look at this," said Jake.

"I think you've just made us a pantry!" exclaimed Molly.

"By golly, Molly, I think I have!" Jake grinned. "This could be a perfect place to store snacks."

Then Molly noticed the two-by-four near her pile of cedar shavings. It also had a loose knothole. She pushed on it and—*pop!*—instantly created another pantry.

"Wow! This is great!" cried Molly. "Now we both have pantries!"

"And look!" Jake turned his knot on its side. "These lumps of wood make perfect tables!"

Molly sat down in front of her table.

"I love it!" she cried. "It's like we're two customers in a restaurant!"

"That sounds like a fun game," said Jake. "Want to play?"

"Sure," said Molly.

For a while Molly and Jake played together much as they had when they were young mice growing up in the deli. First Molly pretended to be a difficult customer and Jake waited on her. Then they switched roles and Jake became the troublesome customer. It was the first time in a long time they actually had fun together.

Then Jake got sleepy. "Think I'll take a nap," he said with a yawn, and crawled onto his pile of cedar shavings.

Molly wasn't sleepy yet, so she decided to look out the peephole for a while.

At first all she saw was the greenish glow of the guppies' aquarium on the class-pet table. Then slowly her eyes adjusted to the darkened space and took in the entire classroom. She studied the alphabet above the blackboard where the multiplication tables were written out. She observed every detail of the reading center, the science lab, and the computer terminals. And for a long while she just stared at the artwork and photos on the bulletin board, and watched the papier-mâché mobile of the solar system slowly turn.

It was only a few hours past midnight, but already she couldn't wait for the school day to begin. She felt like someone sitting in a theater staring at an empty stage, wishing the show would start. One by one she went down the rows of desks and chairs, now buttered with moonlight pouring through the windows, and tried to remember who sat where and what their names were.

"Now let's see. That's where Nancy sits and that's . . ."

Just then Gino stuck his head through the wall.

Chapter 5

Oh my! You startled me," cried Molly.

"Sorry," said the old ghost as the rest of his body slid into view.

"Where have you been?" asked Jake with a yawn. "Hamster Heaven again?"

"No, just checking around to make sure there were no open windows where Big Gray could get in."

"Were there?" asked Molly nervously.

"No, but there was an exhaust vent open."

"There was?" gasped Molly. "I hope you closed it!"

"Tight as a small collar on a big dog's neck," said Gino. "But that's not why I dropped by. I found some nesting materials I thought you two might be interested in."

"Yarn?" guessed Jake.

"No, but it's just as soft. Maybe softer," said Gino.

"Softer!" squeaked Molly. "Oh, tell us! What did you find?"

"Cotton," said Gino, "fluffy white balls of pure cotton. There's a whole jar of them in the nurse's office. Are you interested?"

"Cotton!" Molly's tail danced like a happy snake. "Oh, we'd love some cotton for our nests! Wouldn't we Jake?"

Jake knew that, among mice, cotton was

considered to be "The Big Cheese" of nesting materials. Back at the deli he spent days trying to figure out how to open a vitamin bottle, just so he could get at the cotton that was inside. But now, however, all he had to say was, "Cotton, yeah. That's pretty good for nests."

And to himself he grumbled, *First Peaches, then the lovebirds, and now Gino! Whose nest is this, anyway?*

Molly could hardly contain herself. "Cedar shavings are fancy. But cotton! That's luxury. That's the Ritz! How do we get to the nurse's office?"

"Just follow me," said Gino.

Gino led the way down two-by-four studs, over lumps of plaster and lath. Molly followed closely behind, and Jake brought up the rear.

"It's a good thing you glow in the dark," said Molly.

"Why's that?" asked Gino.

"Because it's pitch black inside these walls, and you don't have a scent we can follow," answered Molly.

"Most ghosts don't," agreed Gino. "But I could make myself have a strong one if you like. How about rotten eggs?"

"No, thanks," said Jake, wrinkling his nose. "The glow will do just fine."

From time to time Gino made detours around doorjambs and windows.

"I'm all turned around," said Molly. "It feels like we're going in circles."

"Don't worry. You'll get the hang of wall travel,"

said Gino. "It takes a lot of practice, but it's worth the trouble."

"How would you know?" asked Jake. "You lived your whole life in a cage."

"Actually, that's not true," said Gino. "Early on, I escaped from my cage and lived in these walls for several weeks."

"How did they catch you?" asked Jake.

"Catch me?" replied Gino. "Nobody caught me. I was as quick as a minnow back then! I turned myself in."

"Because you missed the kids?" asked Molly.

"You bet," said Gino. "I missed them terribly."

"It must be fun to get picked up and held and petted," said Molly. "I'd love to be a class pet. Even if it was just for a day."

"And live in a cage?" cried Jake. "I'd rather lose my tail in a mousetrap!"

Directly ahead of the trio was a faint light.

"Almost there," said the cheerful ghost.

The light came from an open air vent that looked down into the small, square room that was the school nurse's office.

As they approached the vent, Jake sniffed. "Smells like Band-Aids and rubbing alcohol."

Molly looked down through the grate and saw only the black-and-white pattern of the tile floor beneath.

"That's a long way, straight down," she squeaked. "We'll break our necks if we try to jump that far."

"No problem," said Gino as he floated through the grate. "I'll lower you down."

As he descended, the grate cut through Gino's body like an egg slicer cuts through an egg.

"Just crawl through the grate and hop down onto my back," said Gino hovering beneath the vent.

"I can crawl through this grate all right," said Molly. "But you're a ghost. If I step on your back, I'll fall right through you!"

"Not if I don't want you to," said Gino. "Go ahead, try it. You'll see."

"I wouldn't, if I were you," cautioned Jake.

Molly hesitated.

"Well? I'm waiting," called Gino.

"Okay," said Molly, and she lowered her body through the grate and waved her tail around until it touched Gino's "body."

"Hurry up," said the old ghost. "Making myself dense uses up lots of ectoplasm."

"What's *ectoplasm*?" asked Molly.

"It's what we ghosts use to make ourselves solid," said Gino impatiently. "Come on!"

Holding on with her front paws, Molly lowered her legs onto Gino's back.

"That's good," said Gino. "Now the front paws."

Molly let go and allowed herself to drop all the way through the grate.

"Good. Now hold on," said Gino, and he immediately began lowering Molly down to the floor.

What an odd sensation, thought Molly. Gino's fur felt like real fur. But his body was cold. When they reached the floor, Molly quickly jumped off.

"You okay?" asked Gino.

"Just fine!" squeaked Molly.

29

"Wait right here. I'll go back and get Jake," said Gino, and he lifted straight up toward the ceiling like an elevator.

"Sorry, no pony rides for me tonight," declared Jake as he stepped back from the grate.

"But you just saw how easily Molly did it," coaxed Gino. "Just hop down onto my back, and I'll lower you to the floor in no time."

"No way!" said Jake. "I'm not going."

Gino looked up and studied Jake's face through the crisscross of the metal grate. He saw many emotions in Jake's eyes, but mostly he saw fear.

"I won't drop you," said Gino. "I promise."

"You say that," said Jake. "But how do I know you won't run out of ectoplastic?"

"It's ectoplasm," corrected Gino. "Don't worry. I know what I can do and what I can't do."

"So do I," said Jake. "You and Molly can get all the cotton you want. I'm going to look for something *softer*."

When Molly heard this, her ears nearly dropped off.

"Jake, have you gone crazy!" she squeaked. "There's nothing softer than cotton for nest building! And you know it!"

"You can bring me back some cotton if you want," said Jake. "But I'm not going through that grate. And that's final!"

Now Gino recognized the other emotions that showed in Jake's eyes. It was like looking into a cauldron of emotional soup. And it was a soup that needed to be left alone to simmer, not stirred.

31

Molly could sense some of this as well.

"Jake, are you okay?" she called up to her brother.

"Yeah, I'm fine," said Jake. "I just want to go exploring on my own for a while."

"You don't sound fine," commented Molly.

"I'll meet you later, back at the nest site," said Jake.

"Okay," said Molly. "Just one thing . . ."

"What now?" Jake heaved a long sigh.

"Don't forget about Big Gray," said Molly. "Okay?"

"I already promised I wouldn't go outside!" snapped Jake, and he disappeared into the darkness without saying good-bye.

Chapter 6

"I hope you don't think badly of Jake," said Molly when Gino reached the floor again. "He's not always so moody."

"I'm used to dealing with moods," said Gino. "That's a lot of what being a class pet is all about. Sometimes kids don't get much attention at home, but we class pets are *always* there for them. All they have to do is open our cage doors and reach in. Sometimes just having someone warm and furry to hold makes all the difference. So I know about moods. I know a lot about moods."

"Too bad nobody wants a house mouse for a pet," said Molly. "I know I'd be a good one."

"Stick around long enough and you may get your wish," said Gino. "Stranger things have happened."

"That's the problem," said Molly. "Jake only agreed to stay at P.S. Forty-two if he likes it. If he decides to move on, then I have to go with him."

"Couldn't you stay on your own?" asked Gino.

"I guess I *could*," said Molly. "But when we left the deli we both promised our parents we'd stick together, no matter what."

"Ah . . ." Gino nodded his head slowly up and down. "Now I see. . . ."

Molly wished Gino would say more. But the old

ghost, who never seemed to be at a loss for words before, remained silent.

Finally Molly sighed. "If only Jake could learn to like kids more. Then he'd see how much fun it could be living in a school."

"Don't give up," said Gino. "Things change when you least expect them to. Take me, for example. One day I was too old and feeble to play much with the kids. The next day I woke up dead! Dead and spry as ever!"

"Thanks for the encouragement," said Molly. "But waking up dead is not my idea of a cheerful thought."

"I know one thing that will cheer you up," chuckled Gino.

"Really," said Molly. "What's that?"

"Cotton!" said Gino.

"Oh, yes! I almost forgot!" Molly looked around. The nurse's office wasn't much bigger than a large closet. There was a desk, a chair, a cot, a scale, a flag, a tall wooden cabinet, and not much else. "So where is this cotton you've been talking about?"

"Right there!" Gino pointed to the cabinet. "On the shelf."

Molly stared at the cabinet door.

"Huh?"

"Silly me!" chuckled Gino. "I forgot you don't have X-ray vision." Gino laughed so heartily a few of his ghost hairs fell to the floor and disappeared like snowflakes on a warm tongue.

"X-ray vision?" said Molly. "Like Supermouse?"

"That's right," replied Gino. "We ghosts can look inside of *anything* we want to."

All of a sudden Molly felt as transparent as water. "Even me?"

"Even you," said Gino. "For ghosts the whole world is made of glass. The glass can be thick and cloudy, or as thin as a soap bubble. It's all a matter of focus."

Molly scratched her head and looked puzzled.

"But, Gino, I can't focus on what's inside the cabinet unless someone opens the door."

"You can with X-ray vision," said Gino. "Just close your eyes and I'll give you what we ghosts call 'The Gift of Deep Sight.'"

Molly felt eager and scared at the same time. The Gift of Deep Sight sounded neat all right. But what if Gino didn't know what he was doing? What if something went wrong and she went blind?

Molly closed her eyes and then opened them again.

"This isn't going to hurt is it?"

"Not at all," said Gino.

Molly's eyelids lowered a second time, and Gino spoke softly in a low voice, "Deep eyes, be wise, deep eyes, be wise . . ."

Then he touched Molly's forehead with his nose.

"Have you started yet?" asked Molly.

"I just finished," said Gino as a big smile spread across his face.

"I don't know why you're smiling," said Molly. "It didn't work. All I see is you. Not inside of you."

"But, Molly," said Gino softly, "your eyes are still closed."

"What!" Molly reached up and felt her own eyelids.

35

They *were* closed! She quickly opened them and looked around. "Oh mouse! That was really weird! I saw through my eyelids!"

"That's right," said Gino. "Like I said, it's all a matter of focus."

Molly was still confused.

"But I am focusing. I'm focusing just fine. How come I'm not seeing through anything now?"

"That's because you're not focusing *into* anything right now," said Gino. "You're focusing *at* things."

Molly sat back and threw up her paws.

"You just need a little practice that's all," said Gino. "Let's start with the cabinet. Look at that."

"Okay," said Molly. "I'm looking at the cabinet."

"Good," said Gino. "Now focus your eyes—well, your *mind* really—on what's inside the cabinet and tell me what's there."

"How am I supposed to know that?" answered Molly. "The door is shut!"

"You don't have to *know*," said Gino. "Just *imagine*. Imagine what you *would* see if the door were open."

"You mean just pretend?" said Molly.

"Precisely!" exclaimed Gino. "All magic starts there."

"Okay. In that case, I see a jar of cotton balls . . ." began Molly. "That's what you said, right?"

"Right," said Gino. "What else? What else would you guess was in there?"

"Band-Aids?"

"What else?"

"Well, I see a pair of scissors and a tray full of paper clips and . . ."

Suddenly Molly's jaw dropped so low an ant could have crawled over her bottom lip. "Oh my! . . . I see *everything!*"

"Everything?" Gino beamed a smile so big and broad it slipped off his face. For a brief moment, it hung in midair like a Cheshire cat smile.

"Yes! Yes! I see everything right through the door! I see the glass jar of cotton balls on the middle shelf! It has a metal lid. I see two tubes of white cream and a blue bottle and a jar with popsicle sticks. . . ."

"Those would be tongue depressors," said Gino.

"And I see a box of pencils, and plastic gloves, and . . ." Molly rattled off everything she saw, including a housefly that had gotten trapped inside the cabinet earlier in the day.

"Fly? What fly?" said Gino. "I don't see any fly."

"Top shelf," said Molly.

Gino stepped a little closer to the cabinet. "Oh yes, now I see the little critter. My X-ray vision is a little off: maybe . . . twenty/thirty. But yours is perfect: twenty/twenty!"

Chapter 7

"I never needed any help building my own nest when we lived in the deli," grumbled Jake as he stumbled through the dark. It was so pitch black inside the walls of P.S. 42, even his large mouse eyes, designed by nature for night vision, were of no help to him. There wasn't much to smell, either. Just wood and plaster. So Jake was forced to rely on his whiskers to guide his steps.

"Molly is having such a jolly time! Doesn't she know that each and every one of Miss Clark's kids could grow up and be a mouse hater—or worse yet, a mouse killer?

"Molly wasn't gaga about kids when we lived in the deli! No, she was sensible then. But everything's changed since we've come here. If you ask me, it's those darn class pets! That fat rabbit, those wacky lovebirds, and that creepy ghost! They're to blame! Living in cages has warped their minds. And now Molly's becoming one of them," ranted Jake as he squeezed between some plaster and a wooden beam.

"I have to get Molly away from here. But first I'll show them who knows how to build a nest! That's what I'll do! *Ouch!*" Jake bumped his nose on a sharp nail. "And you!" Jake spat at the nail. "Who said you could poke me like that? You pinhead klutz!"

Jake stopped and sat back on his haunches to rub

his nose with his paws. That's when he noticed the glint of light off to his left.

"Mmmmmm . . . what's that?" He stood up and walked toward it.

The light came not from a vent, but from a crack in the outer brick walls of P.S. 42.

"This school is falling apart," thought Jake. "Deli Dan would never allow a gaping hole like this in his building! He'd fix it right away."

After breathing all the stale air inside the wall, Jake could not resist poking his head out the crack. Like a deer drinking at a fresh mountain stream, he took a sip, then a gulp, of sweet-smelling night air.

"Too bad I didn't notice this crack last night when I had so much trouble getting in," thought Jake. "It makes a perfect mouse doorway to the outside."

It was very late. The streets were quiet and the playground was perfectly still except for one thing: A large fluffy white feather was drifting in the breeze near the jungle gym.

"Cream cheese and crackers!" squeaked Jake. "What could be softer than a feather? That's just what I need for my nest!"

Leaning out the crack, Jake sniffed the night air for any scent of danger. *No sign of that ugly puss!* he assured himself. *Good!*

Jake was ready to jump down out of the wall and fetch the feather when he remembered his promise to Molly.

That sister of mine is always messing things up!

He hesitated, but only for a moment.

Well . . . not this time! Besides, it's not like I'm

really going outside. I'll just snatch that feather and hop right back.

Jake let himself drop out of the wall and onto the blacktop. It was an easy jump. Just one stretch and *plop!* He was down.

Here I come, my beauty!

The feather was slowly descending in a graceful arc.

This is going to be soooo easy! Like taking cheese from a sprung trap.

Jake sat up and raised his paws.

"Come to Poppa!" he coaxed. "Come to Poppa!"

Up close the feather seemed to breathe as it trembled in the cool night breeze.

Jake could almost taste its softness. But as he reached up to pluck the feather out of the air, a sudden gust lifted his prize, his treasure, over his head.

"Rats!" cried Jake as he jumped up and pulled down a pawful of empty space.

Now the chase was on. Concerns for his own safety far from his mind, Jake followed the lovely white feather across the playground. Time and time again it dipped low, and then soared high as if mocking him.

"You'll never catch me!" it seemed to taunt him.

Suddenly, as if tired of the game it was playing, the feather dropped. Down, down, down it fell, gently rocking back and forth, sawing the night in two.

"Now I've got you!" Jake leaped up, snatched the feather out of the air and clutched it to his chest.

"Ahhhhh! Success!" Jake nestled the feather against his chin and whiskers. It was the softest thing he had ever felt. Softer than yarn. Softer than cotton.

Softer than silk! Softer even than his Momma's good night kiss when he was a baby.

"Now they'll see what kind of nest I can make!" declared Jake. "*This* will show them!"

That's when Jake noticed that he was standing in a shadow. Something had come between him and the moon. *How can that be?* he wondered. *A* shadow *in the middle of a playground?*

Jake looked up and studied the shape of the shadow etched on the asphalt.

What are those two pointy triangles on top? he wondered. *They look like cat's ears. But I would have smelled a cat.* Then Jake remembered bumping his nose on that nail in the wall. *Could that . . .*

Jake turned and found himself staring at a mountain of matted gray fur.

Oh, I hope this is not who I think it is!

Slowly Jake raised his gaze and saw the glaring yellow eyes of the hugest, meanest cat he had ever known: Big Gray.

Chapter 8

I can't wait to show Jake my X-ray vision," exclaimed Molly. "He'll think I'm turning into Supermouse!"

"Errr . . . um!" Gino made a noise as if clearing his throat though, of course, being a ghost, he didn't really have a throat. "Sorry to disappoint you, Molly. But the gift I just gave you will, most likely, disappear soon. It's probably fading as we speak."

Molly quickly checked. Gino was right. Already the door to the nurse's cabinet was starting to cloud her view of what was inside.

"Why does it have to fade?" she complained.

"Darned if I know," said Gino. "Magic happens. Then it doesn't. Life is ninety percent mystery you know. Maybe a hundred percent when you really think about it."

"But there *must* be a reason," said Molly. "Am I doing something wrong?"

"No, not at all," said Gino. "Some gifts aren't meant to last, that's all."

Just then the lovebirds flew in through the narrow window above the door to the nurse's office.

"There you are!" squawked Princess. "We've been flying all over the school looking for you!"

Clasped in Princess's feet was a strand of yarn. It stretched out behind her like a long pink jet trail.

Prince also held a strand of yarn, only his strand was bright blue.

"Where's Jake?" asked Prince as he dropped to the floor beside Molly. "I can't wait to see the look of surprise on his face when we show him this yarn."

Princess set herself down beside her mate. For more than a few seconds after the lovebirds landed the yarn continued to fall to the floor in two neat piles of pink and blue loops.

Molly was overwhelmed with gratitude.

"This is for us?"

"But of course, my dear!" cooed Princess as she tucked in her wings.

"We found it on the top shelf in the art room," said Prince. "You're pleased, aren't you?"

"Oh, yes," exclaimed Molly. "You have no idea how thrilled I am. And I'm sure Jake will be too."

"Where is that brother of yours?" inquired Princess.

"Exploring inside the walls," answered Molly.

"What a brave fellow," said Prince. "I'd never go inside a wall, not for all the birdseed in Budapest!"

"And Jake would never leap off a tall building," said Gino. "That's the difference between a bird and a mouse."

"Gino just found us some cotton balls for our nests," said Molly. "Isn't that grand?"

"Grander than a gander!" exclaimed Princess. "What would we do without our dear Gino?"

"Would you like us to fly your cotton back to Miss Clark's classroom for you?" inquired Prince.

"Could you?" asked Molly. "That would speed

things up so much. Gosh, with your help we might finish our nests tonight! It would be so nice to wake up tomorrow with a warm nose."

"Let's get busy then," said Gino. "The first thing we have to do is unlock that cabinet."

"It's locked?" said Molly. "You never mentioned that."

"Is it a big problem?" asked Prince.

"Not if we can find the key," said Gino, turning to Molly. "Can you see it?" he asked with a wink.

Molly's first impulse was to scan the nurse's office with her normal vision. But all she could see from the floor was the underside of the nurse's desk. Then she understood what Gino's wink was all about.

Silly me, she thought, and focused her X-ray vision. Her powers were weaker now, but her gaze could still penetrate the bottom of the nurse's wooden desk.

What a confusing jumble! observed Molly. Paper clips, pens, tape dispensers, notebooks, and bottles of pills were sprawled all around the desk drawers. *They must call her "Nurse Sloppy."*

Then she saw it. In the top left drawer was a metal ring with several keys on it.

"Is that it there, Gino?" She pointed.

Gino had already spotted the key.

"Yep, that's it," said Gino, and he floated up off the floor toward the desk. When he reached the top drawer, he nudged it with his nose, but it didn't open.

"The nurse must have locked it with the master key she wears on a string around her neck," said Gino. "But that's no problem. I'll just use my head."

"Use your head?" asked Molly.

"That's right," said Gino, and he floated over to the tall cabinet that contained the much desired cotton balls.

"Oh, this is neat," said Prince. "I've seen Gino do this once before."

"Gino wasn't kidding when he said he was going to use his head," added Princess. "Just watch, Molly. This is precious."

When Gino reached the keyhole beneath the handle of the door, he paused. Then he closed his eyes and slowly pushed until his head disappeared into the keyhole. He pushed as far as his shoulders. Then he floated backward, withdrawing his head—only his head wasn't his head anymore. It appeared to be made of metal and was shaped like a key.

"Weird, isn't it," said Prince.

"What's Gino doing?" asked Molly.

"He just made a key to open the cabinet door," said Princess. "Now he's going to use it."

Slowly Gino thrust his head, now a key, back into the slot. This time, with a slight wiggle, he slowly rotated his body about forty degrees. And the door to the cabinet swung open.

Chapter 9

Big Gray's eyes stared down at Jake like two hot corkscrews.

"Ahhhhhhhh! . . . What a pleasant surprise," said the sinister feline with a snarl. "If I had known I was going to meet up with you, I wouldn't have eaten any kitty chow before I left the house tonight, and kept my appetite as sharp as *these*!"

Big Gray lifted his right front paw and extended four razor-sharp claws. To Jake it looked like the giant cat was holding a fistful of open pocketknives.

"But I am so glad to see you!" Big Gray flexed his cutlery. "Now we can have some *quality time* together. Just you and me."

There was no time for Jake to plan a distraction. No time to even think. He just started talking.

"Well, I was expecting to see you," he said, looking down at the feather in his paws. "In fact, I brought you a present."

This comment caught Big Gray completely off guard. When his eyes narrowed with puzzlement, Jake seized the moment and thrust the white feather into his face.

"And here it is!" he cried.

The tip of the feather went right up Big Gray's nose.

Overcome by a sudden urge to sneeze, the huge

cat jerked back his head and opened his mouth, revealing astonishingly large, white teeth.

"Ahh . . . ahhhh . . .ahhhh . . ."

"Hey, you!" He stifled the sneeze for a moment. "Stop that!"

But Jake kept thrusting the feather forward until . . .

"Aaaaahhhhh-chooooo!"

Jake shot across the playground like a bullet. But Big Gray was close behind. His padded paws pounding on pavement sounded like thunder in Jake's ears.

Jake ran as fast as he could. But he knew every stride Big Gray took equaled twenty of his own.

If I survive this, I'm definitely going on a diet! thought Jake.

What Jake needed was a place to hide. Then he saw it. Someone had left an empty ketchup bottle on the playground. *To help choose up teams? To play spin the bottle?* Jake didn't care. He was just glad it was there. *If I can just make it to that bottle . . .*

Big Gray was rapidly closing the gap. Then there was no gap. As two giant paws came down on either side of him, Jake launched himself into the air. The jump had to be perfect. And it was! When Jake came down, his head was sticking in the mouth of the ketchup bottle. With one single motion he sucked in his belly and squirmed inside.

Made it!

There was still some old ketchup in the bottle. All dried up now, it stuck to Jake's fur like dark red grease.

"Mouse in a bottle, how appetizing!" Big Gray sneered, trying his best not to appear disappointed.

"Come in here and say that! I dare you!" quipped Jake.

"Feeling bold are we?" Big Gray peered through the neck of the bottle with first one eye, and then the other.

The feline hunter considered thrusting his paw into the bottle. But just thinking of the giant hair balls he would have to cough up from licking all that dried ketchup off his furry paws made him gag. *I can always try that later if all else fails,* he thought. *As long as I get my mouse in the end, it doesn't matter how long it takes.*

Jake was doing his best to follow his poppa's advice and never show fear when dealing with a cat. But he knew his situation was grim. *I'm safe for a while,* he thought. *But how am I going to get out of here? I can't live in a bottle!*

As Jake pressed his back against the glass he was reminded of an old movie he once saw when he lived at Deli Dan's. The movie was called *"20,000 Leagues Under the Sea."*

It's almost like I'm in that submarine and Big Gray is a giant octopus trying to get at me. That's what this is like! Suddenly Jake had all the courage and confidence he needed, because now he was no longer a frightened mouse cowering in a ketchup bottle. He was Captain Nemo, commander of the submarine *Nautilus*!

"Well, mates," Jake addressed his make-believe crew. "Looks like we've got some rough sailing ahead. But have no fear. I, Captain Nemo, will save your salty hides!"

Suddenly Big Gray broke into a purr.

"No need to talk to yourself," he said in a smooth, silky voice. "You can come out here and talk to me."

"Just because I'm smaller than you, doesn't mean I'm *stupid!*" replied Jake.

"No, really," said Big Gray, continuing his pathetic attempt at trickery. "The moon is so pretty tonight. You can't really appreciate *how* pretty from inside that *messy* bottle. Why don't you come out here, and we can watch it together. I never really meant to hurt you, you know. I just like to chase mice. I'm overweight and it's good exercise."

"If you're trying to be clever, it's not working," said Jake. "There's no way I'm coming out of this bottle until you go home."

At the mere mention of the word *home* Big Gray's eyes narrowed.

"Home!" he sneered. "Don't talk to me about home!"

"Why not?" asked Jake. "Don't you like your home?"

"I despise it!" snarled Big Gray. "The whole place smells like soap! Whenever there's fish for dinner, all I get are the bones. And those pesky grandchildren that come to visit think my tail is a handle!"

"You hate kids?" asked Jake.

"Worse than baths," sputtered Big Gray. "Especially the little girls. All they want to do is to hug and smooch me. Ugh! Kiss, kiss, kiss! Hug, hug, hug! Pet, pet, pet! It makes me want to *Kill, kill, kill!*"

Suddenly Big Gray thrust his paw toward the bottle and Jake pulled back.

"The giant octopus is attacking!" cried Jake.

But Big Gray only meant to set the bottle rolling. As it careened across the playground the big cat padded just a few paces behind.

Jake tried to run with the roll of the bottle, but he kept tripping over clumps of dried ketchup. Like clothes in a washer he tumbled head over paws, turning somersaults with each revolution of the glass. When the bottle slowed, Big Gray caught up and gave it another shove.

"If only we had a weapon, we could harpoon that giant!" called Jake to his crew.

Then Jake saw what Big Gray was up to. One end of the playground was several feet higher than the street. Big Gray was rolling the bottle toward that drop-off.

"He's going to smash us on the sea bottom!" cried Jake. "Abandon ship! Through the escape hatch! Every mouse for himself!"

But it was too late. Big Gray had rolled the bottle under the chain-link fence and through the parking lot to the edge of the wall.

"We're sinking into a deep sea crevasse! Davy Jones's locker, here we come!" cried Jake as the bottle rolled over the edge and plunged toward the concrete sidewalk.

Chapter 10

All that remained to get at the cotton was to remove the metal lid from the glass jar.

As Molly began to think of ways to pry it off, Gino called out, "Watch this!"

Gino slowly raised his paws and the lid lifted into the air. As if directing the movements of an invisible crane, Gino turned his paws to the left. Slowly the lid also moved to the left. Then Gino lowered his paws, and the lid gently came to rest on the shelf.

"It's called 'telekinesis,'" said Gino. "Want to try it?"

"I think one magic trick a night is enough for this mouse," said Molly. "Right now I just want to feel that soft cotton on my face!"

Molly leaped onto the rim of the jar and peered down inside. It was like looking at a pond of lovely white water. Yearning to soak in its softness, Molly leaned forward and let herself tumble inside.

"Ahhhh!" she squealed as she bounced into the cotton. "This is heaven!" Molly rolled in the cotton, letting its softness touch every part of her.

"Actually, heaven's not much like cotton," said Gino. "It's more like silk or satin."

Just then the lovebirds flew to the rim of the jar.

"Tell us, Molly, what's your favorite time of the day?" asked Princess.

"Gosh, I don't know," replied Molly. "What's yours?"

"We both love morning best," answered Prince.

"Especially when we've been in our cage all night under our blue cloth," added Princess.

"All birds love morning," said Prince. "It means the end of a long cold night. The return of sun and warmth. Roosters crowing, newspapers landing on front steps . . ."

"And don't forget Miss Clark's kids." Princess nudged Prince with her beak. "That's what it means most of all to us!"

"Yes! That's right," agreed Prince. "Morning means that soon they'll be streaming into the classroom ready to start a new day."

"Why are you telling me all this?" asked Molly.

"Because it's almost morning," replied Prince.

"What? It can't be!"

"If you don't believe us, look out the window," said Princess.

Molly turned to look out the tiny window in the nurse's office. It was still nighttime, but the sky was more blue than black.

"Hey, Gino!" cried Molly. "Look out the window!"

Gino was floating in a trance in the center of the nurse's office as he recharged his ectoplasm.

"Holy fish food!" he cried when he woke and saw how late it had become.

"If we're running out of time, maybe we should forget about my cotton," said Molly as Gino helped her climb out of the jar.

"Don't worry. We still have enough time to get your cotton if we work fast," said Gino.

Prince and Princess quickly flew the two long strands of yarn from the floor to the cabinet shelf. Then Gino got inside the jar and tossed out the cotton balls one by one.

"Can you two birds help Molly tie up the cotton balls with yarn?" asked Gino.

"Sure thing," said Prince, lifting a foot and flexing his four toes.

Just then Molly's nose drew her attention to a glossy magazine the school nurse had left lying open on the shelf.

What a fantastic smell! she thought.

One thing Molly could not resist was a new smell. She knew she should keep working, but she walked over to the magazine anyway.

The magazine was called *Looks.* The open page showed a slim woman in a shiny evening gown leaning against a sleek sports car.

"Now is no time to be looking at a perfume ad," cried Gino. "It's almost morning!"

"Sorry," said Molly, but she couldn't take her nose off the ad, especially the little scratch-and-sniff square at the bottom of the page. When she brushed her paw against it and inhaled, she was instantly transported to a place of great loveliness: a deep inner space where clouds of cherry blossoms hovered in a caramel sky.

I must *have this!* thought Molly, and she quickly tore out the tiny square and brought it over to where Prince and Princess were waiting for her help.

"Can we wrap this up too?" she asked.

"Sure thing," said Prince, and he added the scrap of perfumed paper to one of the bundles of cotton.

Soon two bundles, each containing about five cotton balls, were ready for transport. A loop on top of the bundle would make it easy to carry.

"You don't think the nurse will notice that we took some of her cotton balls, do you?" Molly asked Gino.

"No problem," said Gino. "I fluffed up the remaining cotton balls. She'll never notice."

"And I just couldn't resist tearing out that tiny square from her magazine," said Molly. "I hope that doesn't get us into any trouble."

"I wouldn't worry about it," said Gino, and he gave Molly a pat on the back.

Prince picked up one of the bundles.

"Not exactly as light as a feather," he commented.

"You're so strong, my dear," said Princess. "I'm sure we'll manage."

"Are you two ready?" asked Gino.

The two lovebirds nodded and touched heads.

"Once again we fly, my sweet," said Prince.

Outside the nurse's tiny window the dark blue sky was turning pink.

"Oh, my!" cried Gino. "It's morning already! I was going to take Molly back the quick way through the halls. But Mr. Hobbs, the janitor, will be opening the front door any moment now." Gino looked very upset. "This is all my fault!" he fretted.

"Don't worry, Gino. We'll think of something." Molly reached over to give Gino a reassuring pat, but her paw went right through his shoulder.

"I have an idea!" said Prince. "Let's fly Molly back to Miss Clark's classroom."

"Fly me?" said Molly.

"Oh, yes! That will work," chirped Princess. "We'll have you back in Miss Clark's room in a jiffy!"

Chapter 11

Instead of smashing on the concrete, Jake's bottle fell with a *clunk!* on an empty orange juice container.

"Neptune be praised," Jake called to his crew. "We've landed on a giant sea squash!"

Big Gray jumped down from the wall and stared at the unbroken bottle. The angry fire pouring from his eyes seemed hot enough to melt the glass, but his words sounded cool, calm, and collected.

"Oh, well," he said, turning as if to leave. "Win some; lose some. See you around, mouse."

"Don't be fooled," cried Jake to his crew. "This is just another lame trick. If anything, I'd say he's just about ready to attack."

Jake was right about that. Big Gray took only two steps. Then he spun around, and like a prize fighter delivering a knockout blow, punched his paw into the mouth of the bottle.

Though Jake had tried to be ready, the attack was so swift Big Gray's paw knocked him flat.

"Gotcha!" hissed Big Gray.

Before he could stand up, Big Gray wrapped his claws around Jake's body. The fact that Jake was a chubby mouse had not gone unnoticed. In his mind Big Gray was already tasting Jake's juicy meat. All he had to do now was pull Jake from the bottle and pop him into his mouth!

But Jake had not been caught totally off guard. At the last possible moment he had filled his lungs with air. Now he let that air whoosh out of his mouth, and without a squirm or a wiggle, *drained* himself, like water, out of Big Gray's grasp. One moment he was locked inside the prison of Big Gray's paw. And the next moment he was free!

Big Gray, to say the least, was astonished. No mouse, he knew, had ever done *that* before. In the split second it took Big Gray to react, Jake scrambled to the bottom of the bottle and slammed his back against the glass bottom, just out of reach.

"Nice try, fat cat!" He gasped, checking himself to see if Big Gray's attack had drawn any blood. "You're pretty fast for an old fur ball, but you know *nothing* about the element of surprise!"

Big Gray gave up pretending not to be angry. His paw was soiled with sticky ketchup and still no mouse!

"I'll get you yet!" he fumed. "You'll see! First I'll eat your tail and feet. Then I'll chew on your bones and sweet meat!"

"Hey, that rhymes! Very poetic!" said Jake. "And you never called me 'sweet' before. How dear of you!"

Big Gray's eyes suddenly looked bloodshot.

"Run that little mouth of yours all you like," he spat. "In a short while it won't matter what you say!"

Big Gray strained to shove his paw deeper into the ketchup bottle. As his claws drew near, Jake pressed his body ever more tightly against the glass.

"Just a little more!" said Big Gray with a grunt.

If I make myself any flatter, I'll turn into a pan-cake, thought Jake.

Soon there was only a hair's distance between Jake and Big Gray's outstretched claws. But Big Gray could thrust no farther.

Sweat dripped down Jake's brow. He had been close to a cat's claws before, but never this close.

"You ought to have your nails done," he said. "They look a little jagged!"

"Shut up!" hissed the frazzled cat, and he pushed even harder. He pushed and grunted until the neck of the bottle almost cut into his flesh. Finally a curtain of gloom fell over Big Gray's face.

"Okay, I can't get you that way," he huffed. "But I'm not giving up! Not yet. Not by a long shot!" Big Gray flexed his claws one last time. "You're one meal I'm not going to miss!"

"No sense getting yourself all worked up over a meal. Heck, I doubt I'm a whole meal anyway. Just a salty snack. I certainly feel salty!" Jake wiped some sweat from his brow.

"One way or another I'll get you," said Big Gray. "There's more than one way to skin a mouse!"

"I believe the correct phrase is 'skin a cat,'" said Jake. "But I catch your drift. So what's next, if you don't mind my asking? Are you going to roll me home and put me on a shelf somewhere?"

What's next, thought Big Gray, *is for me to take my paw out of this dumb bottle.*

Big Gray pulled on his paw, but it wouldn't budge. Even when he steadied the bottle with his other paw and tugged with all his might, he could not get free.

The more he struggled, the more his paw swelled.

Suddenly a look of panic came over Big Gray's face.

"Stuck in the bottle now, are we?" said Jake, easing his back away from the glass.

"You're the one who's stuck in a bottle," said Big Gray. "I'm just . . ." He renewed his efforts to free his paw. "I'm just . . ."

"Visiting perhaps? I don't think so!" said Jake. "But don't feel bad. A bottle on the paw is not such a big handicap in life. You can still eat and sleep and do all the normal things cats like to do. And just think of what a neat conversation piece it will be when you're hanging out on the back fence with all your cat friends. I wouldn't be surprised if, after a while, they all want bottles on their paws!"

"But not one with you in it!" Big Gray stood up and tried to jerk his paw loose. Again and again he pulled and twisted and yanked.

"Hey, cut that out!" cried Jake as he was slammed against the glass. Every time Jake tried to stand up he fell over again.

As Big Gray yanked, he pulled the bottle along, spinning it round and round. Scraping against the concrete, the bottle spun, rolled and bumped behind him. Finally Big Gray collapsed on the pavement. All that thrashing about had accomplished only one thing: It had caused his paw to swell and become even more tightly stuck than before.

"That was some dance we just did!" said Jake. "I'm downright dizzy."

"Yeah, well, if I have anything to say about it, that

was your last dance!" snorted Big Gray. "You know what I mean? You're finished. Done! History! End of tale! Game over! Mousemeat!" Big Gray shook the bottle so violently, Jake was jerked off his feet and banged again and again against the glass.

"Hey, cut that out!" cried Jake.

Big Gray had lost it. Even if he wanted to he couldn't stop.

"I said stop it!" cried Jake.

"Look who's giving me orders!" sneered the out-of-control cat.

"I'm not giving you orders," said Jake. "I'm just . . . I'm just . . ."

"Just what?"

"I'm just reminding you that cats like to play with their food," said Jake. "If you kill me now the game is over."

"Anything so I don't have to listen to your squeaky little voice would be just fine with me," hissed Big Gray.

"Okay, I'll shut up. I promise," cried Jake.

"Too late!" Big Gray shook the bottle even more violently than before. "I'm going to shake this bottle till I break your little mouse neck and shut you up for good!"

Now Jake was really scared. Big Gray's eyes bulged like giant black olives, and foaming drool ran down one side of his mouth.

This cat has gone bonkers! thought Jake, and he did the only thing he could think of.

He opened his mouth and chomped down *hard* on Big Gray's paw.

"*Yeeeeeoooow!*" Big Gray screamed and jumped, pulling the ketchup bottle into the air.

Pop!

The bottle slid free from Big Gray's paw and landed beside him with a thud.

Big Gray whimpered like a kitten. The bottle was much cleaner now because all its gooey sticky ketchup covered Big Gray's paw. He licked it once or twice and made a disgusted face. For a moment Jake actually felt sorry for the old gray cat. Then the hard, mean look flowed back into Big Gray's eyes.

The cat stood up and limped over to the bottle. His paw was badly bruised. The hair on his head stuck out in big spiky tufts, and his mouth was twisted in a murderous snarl.

"*No mouse bites me and lives to tell the tale!*" hissed Big Gray. "*From now on you are no longer just prey. You are my* enemy! *As the moon is my witness, I pledge myself to your torment and destruction! And death to all your family and friends, as well!*"

Just then a dark shape loomed over both the bottle and Big Gray.

It was an old man with stooped shoulders and a big plastic bag slung over his back.

"Scat, you mangy alley cat!" The old man shoved Big Gray aside with his boot and reached a dirty hand toward the ketchup bottle. "This is mine!"

Chapter 12

Molly had heard stories of hawks and owls lifting mice into the air. But weren't hawks and owls much bigger and stronger than lovebirds? So much could go wrong. What if the lovebirds crashed, or worse yet, what if *she* wasn't strong enough to hold on?

At the last minute it was decided that Prince would transport the bundles of cotton. And Princess, who was actually the stronger flyer of the pair, would carry Molly.

"Now, here's what we'll do," said Princess. "You're too heavy to lift as dead weight. So first I'm going to fly around the room and build up some speed. Then I'll swoop down and hold out my feet. When you see me coming, just reach up and grab on. Can you do that?"

Molly stretched out both paws and closed them around invisible ankles. "Like this?"

"You got it, honey!" chirped Princess, and flapping her wings, lifted into the air.

By now Prince had gathered up both bundles of cotton, one in each foot.

"I know I can do this if I can just get in the air," he said, spreading his wings.

At first the cotton just slid along the shelf, refusing to be airborne. Prince flapped harder, but still the cotton wouldn't rise.

"Here, let me give you some help with that," said Gino, and he swooped under the cotton and gave it a lift.

At last Prince, with the two bundles of cotton dangling beneath his feet, gained altitude.

"Thanks, Gino! I've got it now!" chirped Prince, and he rose to the narrow window above the nurse's door.

Meanwhile, Princess flew in tight circles, building up greater and greater speed. She was flying so fast, Molly got dizzy watching her go round and round. Then Princess stretched out her wings and broke into a glide.

"Get ready!" she called. "Here I come!"

Molly stood up and stretched out her front paws.

"I'm ready!"

A swoosh of air blew over Molly's face as Princess's skinny legs came rushing toward her.

She didn't remember grabbing hold. All she recalled later was a sudden jerk that snapped back her head.

Then everything became a blur.

"Hold on tight," called Princess. "We're climbing!"

Stroke by stroke, like someone pulling at the oars of a rowboat, Princess lifted Molly higher and higher into the air. So far Molly only knew Princess's gentle, feminine side. But looking up at the muscles bulging beneath Princess's pretty green feathers, she saw how *very* strong this "silly" lovebird really was!

Paws locked like little vises, Molly held on tightly.

Princess seemed confident as she headed straight for the narrow window above the nurse's door. Molly was certain they were going to crash. At any moment she expected to slam into the doorjamb. "If that doesn't kill me, surely I'll die when I hit the floor!"

Molly squeezed her eyes shut and held on for dear life. Princess put all her effort into flying. Bearing down hard, she flapped with all her might.

Then Molly felt the tip of her tail slap against the molding as Princess sailed through the open window.

"We made it!" cried Princess.

"We did?" Molly opened her eyes.

"Yes, and now that we have, perhaps you could loosen up a little on my ankles. You're cutting off my circulation."

Just then Prince joined them and together they flew down the hall.

"Isn't this grand?" cried Princess as she swerved to the left and right for the sheer joy of it.

Molly's tail rippled back and forth like a flag in a high wind.

"I love it!" cried Molly.

"Take it easy, dear," said Prince as he labored with the cotton bundles. "We don't have time for any fancy flying."

"Oh, what a pity!" chirped Princess as she swooped down a stairwell and banked a sharp turn toward Miss Clark's classroom.

Molly thought the ride was *very* fancy, not at all like the mere elevator ride she had taken on Gino's back. That was okay. But this! This was the real thing. This was Flying with a capital F!

"I wish we could soar like this all night," she called up to Princess.

"Some other night we will," answered Princess. "But right now we have to concentrate on landing."

Molly swallowed hard. "Gosh, I hadn't thought about landing!"

"Don't worry," said Princess. "Just let go when I tell you to. You'll be fine."

Down the hall was Miss Clark's doorway. Without slowing down, the lovebirds zipped through it. Then they circled once around the classroom and broke into a glide toward the class-pet table.

"Get ready!" Princess pulled up her wings and dropped her tail.

All of a sudden Molly saw Peaches' cage rushing up toward her. "We're coming in too fast!" she cried. "We're going to crash!"

"Now!" cried Princess.

Blam!

Molly hit the class-pet table with a hard clunk and slid to a stop just a hair's distance from the edge.

Chapter 13

Darn cats!" The old man set down his garbage bag and opened it. "Here I get up in the middle of the night to collect some returnables and what do I find? *Cats playing with bottles!* Who'd believe me? They'd say I was off my meds!" The old man's eyes lit up. "Speaking of meds . . ."

He pulled a flask from his hip pocket and unscrewed the cap. "I wouldn't mind some right now!" He took a swig of cheap brandy and wiped his mouth with the back of his hand. "Arrrggggh! Now I feel better!"

Then he dropped the ketchup bottle into his bag.

Before Jake fell into the darkness, he caught a whiff of the old man's breath.

"Well, gentleman," Jake addressed his invisible crew. "Now we know what it's like to be swallowed by a whale. A smelly whale at that!"

It was pitch-black inside the plastic bag, but Jake could make out all kinds of odors. Mostly he smelled various flavors of soft drink, but there was lots of stale beer and some hard liquor smells too.

The old man picked up the bag and went *crash-clank*ing down the street.

"Cancel the order to abandon ship!" said Jake. "We're probably better off right where we are.

Though I have no idea where this whale is taking us."

It was noisy inside the bag, but the slow, plodding walk of the old man created a rocking motion that soon put Jake to sleep. How much time went by he couldn't say. Sometime later he awoke with a start as the old man dumped the contents of the bag onto the pavement.

"Here you go, Megan," said the man. "I'll just take the cans. They're lighter. You take the rest."

Now Jake could see a young woman wearing a long brown coat standing beside a rusty van. The van had smashed headlights, and cardboard taped over the side windows. Beside the woman stood a skinny boy with red hair.

The old man and the woman bent over the pile of cans and bottles.

"Let me sort too," begged the boy.

"No, Robin, you go back in the van and get ready for school," said the woman. Her voice was soft and gentle, but firm.

"Aww, Mom . . ." complained the boy.

"Go on. Listen to your mom," barked the old man. "Do like I never did."

"You never listened to *your* mom either?" Robin grinned.

"No way! And just look where it got me!"

"You sure have been kind to us, Charlie," said the woman. "As soon as I get back on my feet and get a job, I'll help you get off the street too, I promise."

"Hey, Charlie." Robin picked up Jake's bottle. "Looks like you made a big mistake on *this* one! You can't get nothing back on a ketchup bottle."

"You can't get *anything* back on a ketchup bottle," the woman corrected her son.

"I must have been dreaming," said the old man. "Here, give it to me. I'll throw it in the trash."

At that moment Robin spotted Jake in the bottle.

"That's okay," he said, and quickly yanked opened the van door. "I'll get ready for school now."

Once inside the van Robin did not get ready for school. He sat down on the mattress that was his bed and turned on the naked lightbulb that dangled from a cord above his head.

"Hi, fella," he said, bringing his face up close to the bottle and peering inside. "You okay in there?"

Jake turned to his imaginary men. "Stand down! Stand down! This sea monster seems to be of the friendly sort."

Jake studied the interior of the van. Beside the mattress were two small crates: one full of clothes, the other crammed with books. The "curtains" on the window were made with cardboard and duct tape. There was a thermos and a food cooler. Lots of things hung from the ceiling: shoes, pots and pans, two toothbrushes, a net bag with some onions in it.

This place is more like a mouse nest than a people house, thought Jake.

Robin lay down on his bed still holding the bottle up close to his face.

"Mom says we can't have a pet. But she doesn't have to know about you. Are you hungry? What a silly question. Of course you're hungry."

"As a matter of fact, I'm *very* hungry," replied Jake. "Did you hear that mates? This friendly monster wants to know if we're hungry?"

In a flash Robin was up. He opened the cooler and took out a package of prewrapped cheese slices. Quickly he took off the plastic wrapping and broke the cheese into several small pieces. A few of these he ate himself. The rest he placed in the neck of the bottle and with his index finger pushed them in.

Having lived most of his life in a deli, Jake was a bit fussy about cheese.

"Not my favorite," he said as he lifted a piece to his nose and sniffed. "But don't get me wrong. It will do! It will do just fine!"

As Jake ate, Robin reached under his pillow and took out his plastic dinosaur figures.

"Here's my *Tyrannosaurus rex*," said Robin. "Isn't he cool?" Robin brought the dinosaur up close to the ketchup bottle so Jake could see. "Don't be afraid. He's just plastic."

Jake was not afraid. He was impressed. He'd always loved dinosaurs—ever since he'd seen them in a movie chasing people the same way people chase mice. As far as he was concerned, anyone who had his own dinosaur collection was someone to be respected and admired.

Then Jake burped and Robin noticed.

"Nice burp," said Robin and he swallowed a big gulp of air. "Watch this!" Robin's eyeballs seemed to bulge a little.

Then he opened his mouth and burped loudly. "Not bad, eh?" Robin grinned.

All of a sudden the door to the van slid open and Robin's mother stepped in.

Robin tried to hide the ketchup bottle, but she noticed.

"What's that?" she asked.

Chapter 14

Princess circled round and landed on Peaches' cage. "You okay, Molly?"

Molly lifted her head. She felt sore and her paws ached, but she couldn't stop grinning.

"I'm fine!" Molly beamed. "Really fine!"

"Sorry about the bumpy landing," said Princess. "We'll have to work on that."

"That's okay," said Molly. "The ride was worth it!"

"Hey, you guys!" Peaches woke up squinting from the bright morning light streaming in the windows. "Look what time it is!"

"We were helping Molly with her nest," said Gino's voice. Molly looked around but Gino wasn't there. Just his voice. Then suddenly he appeared, as well.

"It doesn't really matter if Miss Clark catches us outside our cages. But a slip up like this could cost Molly her life," warned Peaches.

"You're right," said Gino. "Pull your head in your cage and I'll lock your door right now."

Before landing on the pet table, Prince dropped the bundles of cotton behind Miss Clark's bookcase. Then he and Princess hopped into their cage.

"It's been a lovely night," said Princess as Gino pulled the blue cloth over their bamboo palace.

"One we'll always remember," said Prince.

Molly rushed over to the lovebirds' cage. "Princess, Prince," she called through the blue cloth. "I just want to thank you for . . ."

"No time for thank-yous," said Gino. "Better hit the road while you still can."

"But I have to tell you all how grateful I feel," insisted Molly. "Momma always said 'A house is not a home without a nest.' But now I know it takes more than a nest to make a home. It takes good friends like all of you and . . ."

"Save it for later!" cried Gino. "Right now you don't have a moment to spare."

"Gino's right," said Peaches. "Hear those footsteps coming down the hall? They belong to Miss Clark!"

"Better run!" called Prince.

"Right now!" chirped Princess.

"Wait a minute," said Molly. "I have more to say. . . ."

"You may never say anything again if you don't hurry," urged Peaches.

"Not a word more!" insisted Gino.

"But Gino," said Molly. "I haven't told you how much—"

"Tell me later!" snapped Gino, and he sent a tiny jolt of electricity to Molly's feet that caused her to leap off the table. Once on the floor she kept going straight for the bookcase.

Just as Molly's tail disappeared from sight, Miss Clark strode into the classroom.

"How are you this morning, Peaches?" inquired

Miss Clark as she dropped a slice of carrot into Peaches's cage. "Here's something I saved from last night's salad, just for you."

After a brief visit with Peaches, Miss Clark removed the blue cloth from the lovebirds' cage.

"Wake up, you sleepy heads," she said, and blew them a kiss.

Only then did Miss Clark take off her coat, shake out her long black hair, and sit down at her desk. Miss Clark was not only one of the nicest teachers at P.S. 42, she was, without a doubt, the prettiest. She wore a dark blue skirt and a white blouse. And today, as it was her custom to always wear at least one article of clothing that was red, she wore a ruby red silk scarf around her neck.

Molly wanted to stay and watch Miss Clark from behind the bookcase. But there was lots of work to be done. All that cotton had to be carried up to the nest site.

Molly carried two balls of cotton at a time. She set aside half for Jake. The other half she added to her own pile of cedar shavings. Then she chewed the pink yarn into smaller lengths and put that on top of the cotton. Finally she took the neat-smelling scrap of paper from the magazine and used it to line her knot-hole pantry.

This is not only the best nest I've ever made, thought Molly with a warm glow of satisfaction welling up in her chest, *it's the best mouse nest I've ever seen!*

Crawling into her nest, Molly suddenly realized how tired she was. Resting her head on the soft cotton, she pulled the yarn around her like a warm pink blanket and closed her eyes.

Molly could feel her dreams tugging at her thoughts. But one thought made her eyes snap open.

Where is that brother of mine? He should have been back hours ago!

Exhausted but unable to sleep, Molly started working on Jake's nest. In a little while it looked more or less like hers. The only difference was the yarn. His was blue. Hers was pink.

Now Jake will have a warm nest to sleep in too, thought Molly as she settled down in front of the peephole.

Most of Miss Clark's students were already seated at their desks. Miss Clark was writing the quote of the day on the blackboard. Today's quote was: "A penny saved is a penny earned."

That sounds like something Momma always said: "Save a bean today. Have a meal tomorrow," thought Molly.

Some teachers at P.S. 42 insisted that their classrooms be "quiet enough to hear a pin drop." But Miss Clark was fond of saying, "Why would anyone in their right mind come to a building full of lively young children to hear pins drop? If I wanted to hear pins drop, I would have stayed home."

Miss Clark, however, did not run a sloppy classroom. Far from it. When the bell rang and Miss Clark turned around to face the class, everyone— no matter what they were doing—sat down at their desks and looked back at her. All this was accomplished without a single word on Miss Clark's part.

Just a look that said, "Time to get to work."

"Who knows who Ben Franklin is?" asked Miss Clark.

Just then Robin walked through the classroom door.

"Sorry, I'm late," he said.

Miss Clark didn't skip a beat. "Just take your seat," she said, and went on with her lesson. Miss Clark never reprimanded students in front of the class when she could avoid it. But she made a mental note to talk to Robin in private about his tardiness.

Robin flashed Miss Clark a toothy smile and almost ran to his desk.

Molly didn't know why, but she couldn't stop looking at Robin. Perhaps it was the way he scanned the classroom when he entered, or the odd way he held his backpack. There was no mistaking the look in his eye; it said, "Don't notice me. I'm up to mischief."

I just know *he's hiding something in his backpack,* she thought. *I wonder what it is.*

Molly watched as Robin sat down, zipped open his backpack and took out his books. This seemed normal enough except for the way he looked around suspiciously to see if anyone was watching him. Satisfied that no one was, he reached into his backpack and quickly slipped a strange object into his desk.

Why am I so concerned about this? Molly wondered to herself. *I should be thinking about Jake. He could be lost or in some kind of a jam. Oh, I hope he didn't go outside!*

Molly couldn't keep her eyes off Robin's desk. Then all of a sudden the desk itself began to *dissolve,* and Molly could see inside it.

"It's my X-ray vision," she squeaked. "It's back!"

Molly squeaked so loudly one of Miss Clark's kids in the back row turned and looked up at the wall.

Then Molly saw the ketchup bottle. And inside the bottle, she saw Jake!

Chapter 15

Jake's nose told him he was in P.S. 42. But it wasn't until Robin took him out of his knapsack that Jake knew for certain he was back in Miss Clark's class.

"This is your new home," Robin whispered when Miss Clark turned to write on the blackboard.

"You got that right," Jake squeaked back.

Thus far Robin had kept the ketchup bottle turned upright. Now, in order to fit it in his desk, he had to turn it on its side. All of a sudden escape became easy.

Great, thought Jake. *Now I can walk out of here anytime I want.*

"I know you can get out now," whispered Robin. "But I guess that's okay. I don't want you to feel like you're my prisoner."

Jake, feeling safe again, no longer felt like playing *20,000 Leagues Under the Sea.* The ketchup bottle ceased to be a submarine and his invisible crew disappeared.

"Oh, well," he sighed. "That was fun while it lasted."

"Everyone knows that Ben Franklin helped write the Constitution," said Miss Clark. "But did you know he once electrocuted a turkey? And did you know . . ."

Robin could see Miss Clark's lips move, but he wasn't listening. He was too busy moving his hands inside his desk. Without taking his eyes from Miss Clark's face, he reached into a jar, took out a peanut, and slid it into Jake's bottle.

I should be leaving now, thought Jake as he brought the peanut to his front teeth. *But only a fool would turn down good grub like this!*

"We used to have a hamster in this class, but he died," whispered Robin. "He liked peanuts too."

While he ate, Jake checked out Robin's desk. It contained all the usual school supplies, but mostly, it was a miniature museum of junk. Bottle caps, paper clips, odd pieces of metal, old computer parts, rubber bands, empty dental floss containers, marbles, and copper wire were just some of the "rare" items on display.

"This kid is a pack rat just like me," said Jake to himself with a smile. When Jake lived at Deli Dan's, he collected salt and pepper packets, toothpicks, twisties, price tags, and green plastic Easter basket grass.

"Okay, class," said Miss Clark. "Let's all take out our math books."

Robin knew exactly where his math book was. While he pretended to look for it, he opened the lid to a cigar box next to the ketchup bottle. Inside the box was a plastic bag full of fluffy white feathers.

"Here's something soft for you to sleep on," he said, and one by one poked the feathers into Jake's bottle.

83

"Feathers!" squeaked Jake. "How did you know I love feathers?"

Several of the feathers were almost as nice as the one that lured Jake onto the playground. Two were just as beautiful and one was even more gorgeous! And they were all so soft and downy. Jake couldn't help brush his whiskers against them.

"Like snow, like warm snow!" He sighed and immediately began piling the feathers one on top of another in the bottom of his bottle.

"Food delivered to my door, an open door at that, and not just one feather, but a whole nest of them!" cried Jake as he set to work. "Holy Swiss! What more could a mouse ask for?"

Then Jake froze.

"Wait a minute." He set down the feather he was about to add to his new nest. "What am I doing? I can't live in this bottle!"

"Why not? You want to, don't you?" replied some inner voice, some other Jake who rarely spoke.

"Yeah, but then I'll be a pet," he answered the voice. "I'll be a *class pet*!"

"What's so terrible about that? You like Robin, don't you?" said the voice.

"I sure do!" replied Jake. "But what about Molly? Who's going to take care of her if I'm living here?"

"You know Molly can take care of herself," said the voice.

Jake picked up the gorgeous feather and thought, *This is the first time a human being has given me anything but trouble.*

Jake had battled with Big Gray in this very bottle. But now the battle going on inside him seemed even more fierce.

For a long time he just sat there holding the feather, wishing he had someone to talk to.

Poppa would know what to do, he thought. Then he shrugged. *But Poppa's not here. I am.*

Finally Jake sighed and crept out of the ketchup bottle.

I sure hope I'm doing the right thing, he thought, and made his way to the opening at the back of Robin's desk.

Robin was busy writing in his math workbook. If he had looked down, he would have seen Jake poised at the edge of his desk looking up at him. But he didn't.

"I hope you don't mind my taking this feather with me," squeaked Jake very quietly. "Don't worry. I plan to pay you back. I can find you lots of paper clips and rubber bands and bottle caps and other stuff for your Junk Museum. I'll just put them in your desk at night, so when you come back in the morning, don't be surprised if you have something waiting for you. And I promise to visit, okay? Just because I have to leave doesn't mean we can't be friends."

With that, Jake adjusted the feather in his mouth and leaped to the floor.

Jake was halfway to Miss Clark's bookcase when Sandra Woods called out, "Eeeek! A mouse!"

Then all pandemonium broke loose. Two boys and a girl dove from their seats. But Jake zigzagged

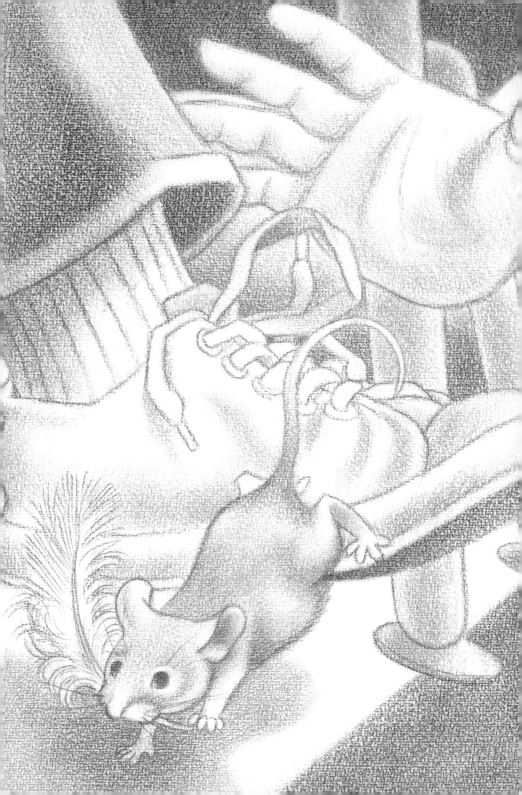

a few times and easily gave them the slip. After being chased by Big Gray, having a couple of kids try to grab him hardly raised his heartbeat.

"Please, everyone back in your seats," said Miss Clark calmly. "Mr. Hobbs, the janitor, will take care of this!"

Chapter 16

Instead of a friendly welcome, Jake got a scolding. "Where have you been all this time?" Molly wanted to know. "I was worried *sick* about you!"

"Just exploring," replied Jake.

"Exploring all night!" squeaked Molly. "Why didn't you check back with me? I didn't know whether to go out and look for you or not!"

"I couldn't," said Jake, and he told Molly most of what had happened that night.

"But you promised not to go outside!" cried Molly.

"Yeah, I know but . . ."

Molly was furious. "And you should have waited till the coast was clear before you jumped from Robin's desk. Now we've got the school janitor on our case!"

Suddenly Jake noticed his new nest. He immediately went over to it and touched it with his nose.

"This is mine?"

Molly nodded proudly.

"Gosh! You did a great job, Molly! Thanks a lot!" exclaimed Jake. "And yarn, too! That's super!"

"You don't mind that I made it for you?" asked Molly. "I know you wanted to make it yourself. But . . ."

A few hours ago Jake would have minded. He would have minded a lot.

"No, I don't mind," said Jake. "It's a great nest. Really."

Suddenly Molly felt calm again.

" I saw you eat the peanut Robin gave you. And I saw how you started to build a nest with all those feathers. You were thinking of becoming his pet, weren't you?"

"You saw that?" said Jake. "How?"

"It's a long story," said Molly. "I'll tell you later." Molly was so tired she could hardly keep her eyes open. "I have to go to sleep now."

Molly crawled into her nest and pulled the pink yarn around her.

"So *were* you?" She yawned.

"Was I what?" asked Jake.

"Thinking of becoming Robin's pet?"

Jake considered lying to his sister but he couldn't.

"Yeah, I thought about it," he confessed. "I really did. But I didn't want to leave you here all alone in the wall."

"Because of the promise we made Momma and Poppa?" asked Molly.

"Yeah. It just didn't seem right," said Jake.

"That's good of you," said Molly. "But I wouldn't mind, really. We'd still be in the same building. As far as I'm concerned you can go back and live in Robin's desk anytime you want. I know I would."

"No way," said Jake. "That was just a momentary madness. That's all." Jake crawled into the center of his nest with Robin's feather.

"Does that mean you want to move on?" asked Molly. "P.S. Forty-two is the perfect place for me. But if you don't really like it here . . . if it's never going to be *your* home too . . . Well . . . I won't make you stay."

"Move on? Heck no!" said Jake. "I want to stay."

"You do? How come?"

"Well . . . because . . . errr . . ." Jake didn't quite know what to say. "Because of these nests . . . yeah . . . that's why! Where else could we build super nests like these?"

Jake wasn't lying. But he wasn't telling Molly the whole truth either.

"These nests sure are great," agreed Molly. "No more cold noses for us! But I got the feeling you wanted your nest to be different from mine, and these two nests are more or less the same."

"No, they're not," said Jake.

"How do you figure that?" asked Molly. "Both are made of cedar shavings, cotton, and yarn."

"Yeah, but my nest has a feather!" said Jake as he nuzzled Robin's feather with his nose.

"Yeah, my yarn is pink," said Molly, starting to dream even while she spoke. "And your yarn is blue, true blue, like blue cheese and blue ribbons under a blue moon and . . ."

"Good night, little sister," said Jake.

"Good night, blue brother," murmured Molly.

Jake was tired enough to sleep, but he didn't want to. When he heard Molly's breathing become deep and slow, he quietly climbed out of his nest, crept over to the peephole and began to watch Miss Clark's class.